T0193990

DREAM
MAKERS

DREAM MAKERS

ELMER M. HAYGOOD

DREAM MAKERS

This is a work of fiction. All of the characters, names, incidents, organizations, and dialogue in this novel are either the products of the author's imagination or are used fictitiously.

iUniverse books may be ordered through booksellers or by contacting:

iUniverse
1663 Liberty Drive
Bloomington, IN 47403
www.iuniverse.com
1-800-Authors (1-800-288-4677)

ISBN: 978-1-4917-7208-9 (sc)
ISBN: 978-1-4917-7209-6 (e)

Library of Congress Control Number: 2015911006

Print information available on the last page.

iUniverse rev. date: 07/10/2015

CHAPTER 1

This place looks completely deserted, says Jacob Jones to himself as he and Macie step down from their black Humvee. They are a two-man lead of an army search team of four assigned to find mines and improvised explosive devices on the streets of a small Afghan town. The scene is all too familiar to Jacob—rows of deserted fragments of sod brick buildings that show signs of artillery and small-weapons fire. Now the only inhabitants are foreign soldiers and live explosives buried throughout. The team has been informed of recent enemy activity in the area, which indicates the high possibility of land mines and IEDs. Jacob retrieves his electronic detector from the rear of the Humvee as Macie retrieves his. He then attaches the detector to his arm with the Velcro pads on the handle of the detector. He twists the pads a little and then retightens them.

"I think I've lost another five pounds today in this heat," says Jacob, a robust 220-pounder on a six-foot frame enhanced by combat gear. "You probably haven't lost a pound."

"Want a candy bar?"

"No."

"Of course you don't. You don't want to ruin those rock-hard abs."

"I eat candy bars."

I told you, man—women like their men short and with a little more meat on them, like me. That's why the Pillsbury Doughboy is so lovable."

"Ha! And he wouldn't be if he had hard abs."

"Right."

Jacob puts on his sunshades and looks up momentarily at the searing sun. Then he and Macie swing their instruments from side to side around and under the truck and then make their way to the front. Jacob gives the driver a thumbs-up and then adjusts his shades and looks down the short dirt road ahead. The roads in this town are narrow with about enough space for two Humvees side by side. Jacob can see that the road appears to widen a little in the distance … or maybe that is where buildings have been completely flattened by aerial bombing.

"My dog is ready to hunt," he says.

"Ready!"

Jacob and Macie separate to cover the width of the road. Jacob is the lead, and he positions himself to the left side as Macie moves to the right rear. As they move forward, the Humvee remains motionless until Jacob and Macie have gone approximately fifty feet away. Then the Humvee slowly tracks behind them. Not long into the search the driver can see that Jacob has raised his hand to halt the team. Jacob removes a small narrow shovel from his side and carefully pokes around a suspicious-looking rock. After finding only pieces of scrap metal, he takes a sigh of relief and signals for the search to resume. The team approaches the area that Jacob believed to be a clearing. It appears to have been a courtyard encircled by small buildings but is now primarily a small field of stones. The road continues on the other side for a short distance. As they scan the field of stones, Jacob can see parts of weapons and ammo casings intermingled with the stones.

"Looks like this was some type of meeting place," says Macie.

"Maybe a drone got this one."

"Yeah."

Once they cross the courtyard to the other section of the road, Jacob feels a tap on the shoulder from behind.

"Okay, man. Time to switch."

They pause to relax a moment. They have a ritual that whenever they switch, they will take a few minutes to look around and take a smoke break. Jacob looks at his comrades in the support vehicle and gives the thumbs-up sign as he removes his helmet and wipes the sweat from his forehead with a handkerchief. He can see there is only a short distance more to scan. Macie pulls out a pack of cigarettes from his jacket and steps a few paces away from Jacob.

"You still don't smoke, do you?"

"Nope. I have no reason to start."

"If bombs won't make you start, nothing will."

"I'm working on finishing things."

"That's right. This is your last outing. I believe we're good here."

Jacob nods a couple of times in agreement; however, he is not so confident. He is plagued by the comments of a friend back home who admonished him to be extra careful in the last few months of his final deployment. He remembers that the friend had a relative in law enforcement who was killed in the line of duty three months prior to his retirement. Jacob is finishing the last few months of his final tour of duty. He tries to clear his mind because he needs no additional stressors while searching for explosives. Jacob calculates the remaining distance to be approximately one hundred yards, which is minute compared to the distances they have already covered today. Jacob stares into the distance and tries not to think beyond it. Suddenly fingers snap in his face.

"Are you with us?" asks Macie.

"I'm here. Just daydreaming."

"Yeah! In a minefield! That's just like you. But I can understand. I wish I had only a few months left. I wouldn't be out here, though … or maybe I would be if I was a dedicated grunt like you."

"You're on your way, my friend."

Jacob walks to his position in the rear as Macie takes the lead. After covering about a third of the remaining distance, Jacob slows when Macie stops to step over a large stone in his path and then stops abruptly. Jacob notices that Macie is leaning forward in a rigid stance with his left hand extended back to signal a halt.

"What's up, man?"

Macie does not answer and remains in the rigid position; he thinks about the sounds he heard when his left foot landed. He is sure of the sound of the crunching of a small pile of pebbles behind the rock, but he believes he also heard a click. He removes a small extendable rod from his side and extends it to its fullest. He uses the rod to gently move some pebbles beside his foot and immediately sees a small portion of a land mine that has obviously been buried in a hurry. He then waves his hand to motion for the team to retreat farther away from him. Macie does not hear Jacob take any steps backward, which forces him to motion again more emphatically for him to retreat. Jacob begins a slow retreat and looks back briefly at the driver.

"It looks like a three-man! I'm hot!" Macie lowers his head and murmurs to himself, "How did I miss this one?"

Jacob can see Macie poke again around the heel of his left boot. Jacob reflects on the months of bomb-search training in which the instructor frequently reminded the class of the Russian land mine model MS-3 that litters the battlefield. The MS-3 is a pressure-release antipersonnel mine that is often used in conjunction with antitank explosives. While focusing on detecting the innovative riggings of the improvised explosive devices, the bomb teams are constantly finding these remnants from old wars that have been redeployed in the current battle. Macie realizes that he is standing on not only a mine but a small group of pebbles that are not fixed firmly under his foot. As he struggles to remain motionless, he can feel the slight grinding of the pebbles that is causing his foot to shift.

"Hold tight," says Jacob.

Jacob runs to the truck to explain the situation. "It's a land mine, and he's on it."

"Gee. We can't defuse that," says the driver.

"Well, I was a linebacker. I gotta do my thing."

"You're not fast enough."

"We'll have to see."

Jacob runs swiftly back to his original position and begins to remove his gear. As Macie listens to the items fall to the ground, he realizes what Jacob is preparing to do. He shouts out to him, "No, man, no! It won't work!"

Jacob continues preparing to execute his plan. As he crouches to take his first step, he is blinded by debris from a tremendous fiery explosion that propels him backward into the air. He lands on his back with severe injuries and his uniform partially aflame. He attempts to roll on the ground to extinguish the flames but is able to complete only one full roll. He can faintly hear the footsteps of comrades from the Humvee who rush to his aid as he cries out in excruciating pain, "Medic! Medic!"

At 4202 Castle Drive in a small urban town in eastern North Carolina, Jacob Jones is cradled on the floor of his bedroom by his younger brother, Marcus Jones. Marcus has dashed once again from the recliner in the den to comfort Jacob after another nightmare about combat. Each nightmare ends with the recurring episode of Macie's death and Jacob's plea for medical help. Jacob was released from military service because of his injuries and is now also suffering from post-traumatic stress disorder. The nightmares have progressed to the point that regardless of what he dreams about, an explosion occurs that kills Macie. Marcus tries to get to him quickly so he can realize right away that he has just experienced another nightmare. Whenever Marcus delays, Jacob falls to the floor and rolls in an effort to extinguish an imaginary fire on his clothing and cries, "Medic!" Jacob is slightly embarrassed as Marcus helps him to his feet and readjusts the back brace that he has worn for the past five years. Jacob then walks slowly on his own to bed, and Marcus gathers the bedcovers and places them over him. Jacob turns to his side and pulls the covers to his neck. Marcus walks away a little dejected for being too late to prevent Jacob's collapse to the floor. He has slept in the recliner in the den for the past two years just for that purpose. As he returns to the recliner, he realizes that his efforts constantly compete with his own need for sleep.

"Thank you!" yells Jacob.

"No problem. You don't have to thank me each time."

"Sorry, a combat habit. We're supposed to shake hands too. You know that."

"Good night, soldier. We'll shake in the morning."

CHAPTER 2

The next day is rainy, and Marcus Jones is wet as he returns home from his part-time job as a stock clerk at a local store. He walks straight to the bathroom to dry his head and brush his jacket. He removes the wet jacket and takes a moment to survey the wider and improved bathroom made possible by the additional income he is now providing to the household. As he looks at the handicap railings around the shower and the tub, he is convinced that he made the right decision to reduce his course hours in law school to work and help make those and other improvements for Jacob. After high school Marcus was eager to begin earning money to help his mother with household expenses, but after years of prodding she finally convinced him to pursue higher education, which would eventually result in greater income opportunities. Marcus is now twenty-six and is struggling to complete his final years of school. As he goes to his bedroom to change into some dry clothes, he can hear Mrs. Jones stirring in the kitchen.

Mrs. Jones has listened carefully to his steps in expectation of a hug from behind as she washes a small bowl at the sink.

She stands on her toes to look through the kitchen window to check on the covering she placed over her small newly planted vegetable garden out back. She is a middle-aged woman who was raised in a rural area as a child and has lived her adult life in the urban setting as a result of an early marriage. The unexpected death of her husband forced her to abandon her educational plans in order to work full time and raise her two sons. She left her job as an accountant for an independent insurance firm when Jacob returned home as a disabled veteran. When asked by her cosmetologist if she wanted to dye her hair, she responded she wanted to leave it the color of life—gray. She believes she hears tiptoeing and prepares for the bear hug from Marcus. She then sees the flash of arms wrap around her and feels the squeeze as she leans back in laughter.

"You were waiting on the bear, weren't you?"

"Yes. I remember I had two bears."

"I guess you heard Jacob last night."

"Yes."

"You know, Melissa is working on her master's degree in psychology and she has talked with him about a new program at the VA called cognitive behavior therapy."

"What does that do?"

"It is designed to help him focus on other things when he gets depressed about combat."

"What about the nightmares when he is not awake and thinking?"

"Well, I don't know. Maybe the psychiatrist will find an answer now that he is seeing him a little more. Where is he now?"

"He went for a walk. He said those medications for muscle relaxation and pain makes him sleepy, and he doesn't want to sleep and dream all the time."

Marcus hears a knock at the front door. He opens the door and greets Melissa, his girlfriend, with a hug and a quick kiss. She enters with the usual big smile and the brisk prancing steps of her sleek body—molded by years of competitive amateur dancing. She follows the sounds of dishes and finds Mrs. Jones.

"Hello, Mrs. Jones. Do you need some help?"

"No. I'm just washing the bowl set you and I found at the antique market yesterday."

"They are lovely."

"I decided where to display them, and that's right in the middle of the table in a circle."

"That will look good. Where's Jacob? I wonder if he has any information from the psychiatrist for me to review."

"He always does, but he is out walking right now."

"That's good for him. I want to take Marcus out for a little relaxation too—which, of course, he will deny that he needs. I want to take him to a movie this evening."

"Good luck."

Melissa follows Marcus to his usual place of study. She watches as he takes a book from a desk and slumps into a chair and places one leg across an arm of the chair. This is her first time seeing him in the study mode. She had pictured him in the more formal position of sitting at the desk with a book opened flat on top of the desk.

"Tired?"

"Not really. I have some catch-up reading to do."

"Um. I thought we would catch a movie tonight."

"Tonight? It's Wednesday."

"Yes," she says as she leans toward him with a kiss and slowly pulls the book from his hands.

"Okay. Looks like I will catch up later. What are we going to see?"

"A movie."

Jacob enters the house and sees Marcus and Melissa gathering their jackets to go out. He unzips his jacket, which is wet from the rain, which has now stopped.

"What's up for tonight?" Jacob asks.

"A movie," responds Melissa.

Jacob looks at Melissa and then at Marcus and states, "Try to stay awake, man."

"What?" asks Melissa.

CHAPTER 3

Upon their arrival at the theater, Marcus tries to peruse closely the billboard, but Melissa pulls him by the arm to the ticket window. As she makes the transaction, Marcus tries to find the name of the movie on the board behind the ticket seller, but Melissa pulls him toward the entrance.

"I guess you already know what we want to see," says Marcus.

"Yep."

As they climb the stairs of the theater, they can see fewer than ten people in attendance. Marcus stops near the front as he sees that they have arrived early.

"Previews. I love previews."

But Melissa says nothing and continues to climb closer to the top; Marcus immediately joins her. After the previews Marcus leans forward to stare at the title of their movie and realizes that Melissa has chosen a movie that he calls made-for-female ... no car chases, no criminal violence, and no alien attacks. Marcus prepares himself mentally for a mixed bag of boredom and maybe a little romance. As the movie plays, Marcus decides on how to cope with the moment.

"How was your day?" he asks, with no response. "Did you finish your assignment?" he asks, again with no response. "Did you change your hair? Cat got your tongue?"

"Hush. The movie has started."

He slumps down in the chair with his hands folded in his lap and pretends to be attentive to the movie. Melissa looks at him with a smile and gently guides his head to her lap and then pats him on the side. After a short while she peeks at him and sees his eyes are closed. He is possibly asleep, as she had planned. She gives him a few strokes on the side to indicate to him that he is doing just fine, in case he is awake with his eyes closed. At the end of the movie there is a scene of a man, a woman, and a dog running across a beach and splashing playfully in the water. Marcus raises his head slightly to look at the screen.

"Does anyone really do that?" asks Marcus. "Maybe one day you and I will jog across the beach with our dog."

"I don't have a dog, and neither do you. I don't really like dogs … maybe a cat. "Shh! I believe he is going to kiss her now for the first time."

Marcus sits up and stares at the screen. Then he turns to Melissa. "For the first time?"

Melissa pats him on the leg. "Shh! I don't want to miss the end."

"Oh, really?" No car chases, no shoot-'em-ups, no alien attacks, and this … this is the first kiss. Is this, you know, the first everything?"

"Quiet!"

The kiss ends the movie, and Marcus is quiet as they depart with the other patrons. As they enter the theater foyer, Marcus points to the concession stand.

"Look—some action!"

"Where?"

"Over there. See—a popcorn brawl. See how they viciously jump on top of each other and then pile on in that bin. Now look—the police scoop up the rowdy ones and put them in a box and send them off to jail. Wow."

"I see that, Marcus. I really do. Now we are going outside to see more action, like car chases, violence, and—if we're lucky—maybe a couple of aliens fighting in the sky."

"Cool!"

Marcus has spent most of their time together asleep and feels he needs a way to salvage the night. The movie was an early evening show, and it is now barely nighttime. There is light traffic, and Marcus can see that the shops are still well lighted. He notices a few people walking along the sidewalk on both sides of the street.

"The movie made me a little hungry, with all that action. Do you want to get some coffee and dessert down the street?" he asks.

"Yes. I can handle that action, along with a little window-shopping."

"Shopping? Cool."

She notices a shop right away that has an awning with fancy lettering out front indicating it might be a novelty shop. Marcus can see in her eyes that shopping is going to be the major focus.

"I see where I want to go first."

Marcus tries to determine where she is headed by looking back and forth at her eyes until he is standing under the shop's awning. It is a novelty shop as Melissa had suspected. Melissa points to an item on a display rack in the window.

"Isn't that beautiful?"

"Yes, you are."

Marcus reaches his left arm around Melissa and turns toward her to give her a kiss. As he turns, he notices an elderly woman walking slowly toward them. She is carrying a department store shopping bag full of merchandise in her left hand, and on her right arm is a large purse full of items. It seems she has shopped more than she had planned and now seems to be struggling with her purchases. Marcus also notices someone walking behind her in the same direction. A young man wearing a black hooded sweat jacket is pulling the hood over his head and increasing his pace. The young man suddenly bursts into a sprint directly toward her and snatches her purse. The force sends her and the purchases sprawling on the sidewalk and into the street. The thief continues to run toward Marcus and Melissa. Marcus takes a step forward to intercept him but hesitates and holds on to Melissa until the thief passes. After he passes, Marcus sprints after him.

"No! Marcus, no!" screams Melissa as she trots nervously after him.

The chase began approximately fifty yards from the entrance to an alley between two stores. The thief scurries into the dark alley, and Marcus continues after him. As Melissa approaches the alley, she hears two popping sounds that she believes to be gunshots.

"Marcus!" she shouts, but she receives no answer.

She very cautiously peers into the shadowy alley. She sees someone squirming on the ground and moaning in pain. The person attempts to stand but only manages to get to his knees and then collapses back to the ground. Melissa slowly and tearfully walks into the alley and is able to see the colors of the man's clothing.

"Marcus!" she screams as she rushes to his aid.

She can see in the dim light that his jacket is splattered with blood. She screams for help and falls to her knees to cradle him as he struggles to breathe. As she holds him with one arm, she fumbles in her purse with one hand to find her cell phone. Out of frustration she shakes the contents out onto the ground. She sees the glow of the cell phone as it slides on the ground away from her. She gently places Marcus's head on the ground and crawls to retrieve the phone. As she reaches for it, she hears voices and police radio communication at the entrance to the alley. She also sees the elderly victim point her way frantically as she speaks with two officers. Melissa turns and crawls quickly back to Marcus, who is still struggling to breathe. She calls his name in an attempt to bring him to full consciousness, but she hears only grunts and mumbled words. An officer arrives.

"Are you all right, ma'am?"

"It's Marcus!"

"Paramedics are on the way."

The officer sees the injury and applies pressure to the wound. Paramedics arrive at the entrance, but the alley is too cluttered with broken metal clothing racks and trash bags for the county's emergency rescue vehicle to enter. Melissa sees two paramedics hurry down the alley in the light of the emergency vehicle. They quickly assess the gravity of Marcus's injuries, and one remains with Marcus while the other and an officer rush to the ambulance to retrieve a stretcher. Melissa shivers with tears of grief as she stands and watches the men roll the stretcher down the alley.

"What is his full name?" asks a policeman.

"Marcus Jones."

"You know how to contact his relatives?"

"Yes."

As the paramedics begin to transport Marcus, Melissa turns and gathers her personal things from the ground with an officer's assistance. She then rushes down the alley past the police as they attempt to get more information from her.

"Miss. A few more questions, please."

She continues through the alley and down the sidewalk toward her car, which is still parked at the theater. The police officers' continuous attempts to get her attention are ignored. She finally turns and shouts, "See me at the hospital, please!"

Since the items in her purse were replaced haphazardly, she places the purse on the hood of her blue Chevy Camaro and searches vigorously for the keys. She pauses a moment to look in the direction of the ambulance as the siren fades into the distance. After finding the keys and gaining entry into the car, she screeches out of the parking lot and into the street, which is fortunately free of traffic. She wipes tears from her eyes with her hands and leans forward to see the road ahead. She arrives at the red light of an intersection and considers for a moment going through it, but she realizes the imminent danger. She has stopped partially into the first lane of a multilane intersection with approaching traffic. Grief-stricken, she places her head in her hands and leans upon the steering wheel. She realizes that she must tell Mrs. Jones and Jacob right away. She must tell Mrs. Jones that the son who has been the stabilizer in the household is now on the way to the hospital with life-threatening injuries. Melissa cries out uncontrollably, "Marcus! Jacob! Mrs. Jones! My God!"

Then she searches through her purse for the cell phone. As she finds it, she hears a horn behind her and sees that the light has changed to green. She speeds off teary-eyed with the cell phone clutched tightly to her breast. She arrives at the hospital without further delay but pauses a moment to take a few deep breaths. She contemplates whether to call Mrs. Jones now or after she has received definite information on Marcus's condition. Fear paralyzes her momentarily after she sees Marcus's blood on her arms, on her clothing, and on the steering wheel. She reaches for the glove compartment and obtains tissues to wipe them off. She tosses the bloody tissues to the floor of the passenger side. Then she leans back against the headrest and takes a firm grip on the door handle and quickly exits. As she walks down the parking lot, she can see that the red-and-white ambulance that transported Marcus is still under the marquee of the emergency entrance. The paramedics are putting the stretcher into the rear of the vehicle. She notices that one of them has turned to glance at her as she approaches the sliding glass doors.

When Melissa enters the hospital, Marcus is still in surgery. She finds out immediately from the intake staff that she is not allowed in the surgery suite, because she is not his relative. She calls Mrs. Jones as she walks down the hallway to the emergency room waiting area. She takes a deep breath before hearing Mrs. Jones's voice, but as soon as she answers, Melissa sobs greatly while speaking about Marcus. Melissa can hear the trembling in Mrs. Jones's voice as she asks questions about Marcus's condition—which she is unable to answer. Melissa can hear her yell to Jacob that they must leave immediately for the hospital. Mrs. Jones in a shaky but calm voice tries to comfort Melissa before hanging up.

"Jacob and I will be there soon. Don't try to do anything before we get there."

"I tried to stop him. We could have stayed home."

"No, dear. You did the right thing. We are leaving now."

Melissa composes herself as she raises her head to glance around the room. She is a little disappointed she didn't hold together better while she was speaking with Mrs. Jones. Through tears she tries not to look at the faces of the people who are waiting for treatment or for loved ones. There seems to be an unusually large number of people for the small urban town. She searches for a group of seats to reserve that will offer the most privacy when Mrs. Jones arrives. She hears a patient being called by the receptionist. Three people rise near the entrance, approach the receptionist desk, and then depart. Melissa moves to reserve those seats.

As soon as Melissa sees Mrs. Jones arrive with Jacob, she rushes to embrace her. Before Mrs. Jones can ask the first question, Melissa gently guides them to the chairs she has reserved. Melissa explains that Marcus was shot during a heroic effort to help an elderly victim of a purse snatching and is now in surgery. The dreadful news is overwhelming to Mrs. Jones as she rises in Melissa's arms and walks swiftly to the receptionist's desk.

"I need to see my son."

"Who is your son, and do you have an ID?"

"His name is Marcus Jones, and we are his family. I do have an ID."

"He is still in surgery. The doctor will come out to you when surgery is over. He will meet you in the surgery suite. Go through the waiting area, and you will see a set of double doors to your left that says, 'To Surgery Waiting Area.' You will see a small waiting area to your right as you enter. There will be an attendant in there if you need any help."

"Thank you."

After they enter through the double doors, Melissa walks ahead and opens the door of a small twelve-by-twelve-foot area with a metal-framed glass window. The room faces a similar area across a narrow hallway that is occupied by a man and two women. The rooms have four short rounded and cushioned lounge chairs and a small attached counter area with all the preparations for making coffee; there is a box of tissues beside the coffeepot. As Mrs. Jones takes a seat, Melissa remains standing and looks across the hall at the man, who is seated with his eyes closed and his head leaning back over the top of the lounge chair. The women are seated next to each other holding hands, and they are engaged in a conversation. Jacob stands away from Mrs. Jones and Melissa to stretch and relieve his back. Mrs. Jones motions for Melissa to bring a chair closer to her so they can have a private conversation.

"I've had troubling dreams about my sons, but they always turned out all right. I'm confident Marcus is going to be fine."

As she is speaking with her back to the window, Melissa can see two men dressed in business suits pass by the area and walk down the hall. Soon afterward she sees a nurse approach and enter from the hallway.

"Mrs. Jones, I need to take you to the recovery room."

Melissa and Jacob join them as they exit for the hallway. They enter through a single white door and see an all-white room where Marcus is in a bed. He is surrounded by the doctor and the two men in business suits, who appear to be detectives. One of the men is leaning his head close to Marcus in an apparent effort to hear what he is saying. The nurse informs the doctor and a detective of the family's presence, and they turn to acknowledge them. As the family move closer, the two men prepare to move out. They offer their sympathy for Marcus's injuries and assure Mrs. Jones that all will be done to bring the shooter to justice. After offering Melissa a business card, they depart. Mrs. Jones can now see clearly the four IV lines and the oxygen tubes that enter Marcus's motionless body. She can also see a puzzling display on a heart monitor on a stand beside the bed. The doctor notices her staring at the monitor.

"I'm sorry I couldn't do more for him. The next forty-eight hours is the pivotal point."

"Forty-eight hours? Then what? He is going to make it beyond that, isn't he?"

"It's possible, but it is a very low percentage."

As he pronounces the last few words, Melissa embraces Mrs. Jones from behind. She can feel the strength in her legs begin to wane. Melissa guides her to a chair provided by the nurse. Jacob stands with his eyes closed in disbelief. The nurse assists Melissa in escorting Mrs. Jones closer to the bed, and she asks that only Mrs. Jones speak with him. Jacob and Melissa stand on each side of her and close enough for him to see them. Mrs. Jones forces back tears and places her hands upon his hand. Marcus turns his head slightly to look at her.

"You're going to make it," she says.

Marcus whispers, "You know the light in the tunnel? I've seen it."

Mrs. Jones stares silently at him for a moment and then squeezes his hand as tears flow from her eyes. "Don't be afraid of it. That's where the Master lives. You are a good son."

Jacob quickly interjects, "Hold on, man! You're gonna make it."

As Jacob speaks, Marcus closes his eyes and takes his final breath. Marcus Jones begins his journey through the proverbial tunnel to the light. He sees a silent rotating black tubular passageway with walls of small twinkling lights like stars in the night. He moves along wide-eyed, panting rapidly and bedazzled by the lights. In expectation of meeting the Master, Marcus contemplates on what he will say in that special moment. The light begins to engulf him as he continues to move forward. He falls to his knees, spreads his arms high and wide, and shouts nervously into the blinding light, "Lord, it's me!"

When the blinding light fades and his eyes refocus, Marcus realizes he has arrived on his knees in the midst of a small group of people who applaud and laugh. He notices that he has been clothed in a long-sleeve white shirt and white pants and soft white shoes like everyone else. He also has a small flat rectangular gadget attached to the back of his left hand; it has three buttons, labeled 1, 2, and 3. He flips his hand a few times and realizes the gadget is permanently attached, and he can't figure out how. He is bewildered and looks around at the crowd of smiling faces, which begin to disburse along the rotunda-style foyer to a series of connecting corridors. He slowly stands and sees someone shout and point, "Over there!"

Marcus looks toward a hallway of approximately fifty feet that leads to what appears to be a chamber. He walks slowly along the white marble floors to the opened double doors. He leans in a little and sees people dressed as he is who are seated in seats across the width of an auditorium. A man at the front is speaking to the crowd. When he sees Marcus standing in the doorway, he invites him in.

"Welcome, Mr. Jones. I am the Dream Master. You complete this assembly, and you will find your seat near the rear."

Marcus sees an empty seat at the end of an aisle several rows to the rear. The seat is upholstered with a shiny gold fabric and has an engraved iron end cap painted gold with dark stained wooden armrests. He quickly surveys the other seats and the walls of the auditorium with its carved wooden columns. He looks up to see three large sparkling chandeliers hanging from the ceiling. At the front and behind the Dream Master is a large white viewing screen that is centered and covers most of the front wall. It extends from the ceiling to a few feet above a wooden platform, which is about four feet high. Attached to the viewing screen on one side are four small screens in a vertical row. All the screens appear to be built into the wall. Marcus concludes that, except for the small screens, the whole auditorium is a replica of an early 1900s movie theater. He notices that the audience is silent and many of them have turned to look at him with smiles on their faces. He recognizes several nationalities as they stare at him in complete silence. He turns back to the Dream Master.

"Where am I?"

The question sparks a spontaneous burst of laughter from the crowd and the Dream Master. The audience turns back to the front as they continue to chuckle out loud. Marcus looks at the audience and then turns to the Dream Master.

The Master explains, "We are sorry, Mr. Jones. As an icebreaking activity I asked everyone to time the newest arrivals to see who would take the longest to ask the most obvious first question. You are the last arrival and, congratulations, you are also the winner. For a moment I thought you would just sit down and say nothing."

Marcus forces a brief smile and asks again, "Where am I?"

"And congratulations again. You are also the first to ask twice. I have been waiting for the last person in order to give a onetime complete explanation of what this is all about. You heard the applause from the people in the foyer when you arrived. That's because each of you has received an exclusive selection to be a dream maker. Have you ever awakened one day and said to yourself, 'That was a really weird dream'? Well, if so, that was our responsibility … which is now also yours. You are here to make dreams for the living. I am the

Dream Master for sector 10247 … and you obviously have no inkling of what a Dream Master is. First of all, this is what I look like for those of you who can't see me clearly. It's important that you know the leader of your sector."

Marcus sees the face of a jovial-looking middle-aged man with a slightly plump build. He looks to be of average height with short gray hair and a short gray beard. He is attired in a white top and bottom as the arrivals are, but he also is wearing a plain white sports jacket. Marcus notices his southern accent as he speaks with a big smile with each sentence.

"I assume that you all know this is not a dream. It is the afterlife. I am not a judge, and this is not Judgment Day. I don't sprout wings, horns, or tails. There is another and final phase that you will be aware of later. The Dream Master is, of course, responsible for you, the dream makers who are sent to him from the tunnel. Billions of people lay down to sleep and need dream makers like you. In the very distant past those periods of sleep were moments filled with totally erratic brain activity. The people arose from sleep confused and paranoiac because they didn't understand what had happened to them. I petitioned for that time to be filled with some form of orderly reenactments of life activities that could be remembered in the awakened state."

Suddenly the large screen activates and Marcus sees flashes of a variety of life activities: traffic, kids at play, shopping, sports, police activity, weddings, dancing, funerals, sex, holiday celebrations, and more.

"Do you remember dreaming about any of those things?" He turns back to the audience and continues, "So I was permitted to form the dream makers. Again, did you ever wake up in your life and say, 'That was a very pleasant dream' or 'I had a really weird dream last night'? Well, those dream productions were our responsibility, and I reiterate that they have now become yours as well. They were created in our dream theaters, to which you will be assigned soon in small groups. Now let me demonstrate how all of this works so you can understand what you will be doing in the theaters. The process occurs in two phases. There is the data transfer from the mind of the sleeping person, and then there is the transfer of your composition to the person's mind."

Marcus is stunned by that last statement. He scratches his head and then stands and immediately gets the Dream Master's attention.

"Yes, Mr. Jones?"

"From whose mind?"

"We don't know. We only know that the information we receive here is from those sleeping persons who are assigned to our dream sector. Now, since you are already standing, Mr. Jones, I am assigning you and those sitting beside you as a group and as my volunteers for a demonstration of the dream-making process. All of you should have gadgets on the backs of your hands that control the process. In case you haven't formally introduced yourselves, your group is Marcus, Mary, Sandy, and Miguel."

Marcus steps into the aisle and lets Sandy and Mary go before him. When Miguel comes to the end of the row, Marcus motions with his hand and a nod for him to go also. Marcus begins a quick survey of his team members. Sandy is a petite woman who appears to be barely over four feet but walks with a posture of much confidence. Marcus believes her bushy hairstyle is intended to make her seem taller. Mary appears taller than the average woman, because he can see her head over Miguel's. Then he thinks that maybe it's her slender frame and shoulder-length hair that make her appear so tall. And she is also walking behind Sandy. When they arrive at the front, Marcus notices that he is a little taller than Miguel but perhaps a little shorter than Mary. He notices the rings around Miguel's eyes that are characteristic of someone who wore eyeglasses constantly. The thick mustache makes him appear to be the oldest of the group.

"Mr. Jones, please point your hand to the screen and press button number 1 on your control."

Marcus points his hand, presses button number 1 and watches the large screen change and display the words "Ready to Receive Transmission." He then sees a display on the first vertical screen of what appears to be an excerpt from a movie with no scripted beginning or introduction. The scene is of a fire truck that is traveling down an urban street with its emergency lights activated.

"Now, Mr. Jones, please press button number 2."

The scene is freeze-framed. The second vertical screen activates immediately and displays a woman walking in a wedding gown down the aisle of a large church filled with attendants.

"Now, Mary, it is your turn to select a scene. Please press button number 2."

Mary smiles as she selects the action on the second vertical screen. The third vertical screen activates and displays a house on fire in a neighborhood of luxury homes with well-manicured lawns.

"Sandy, will you please press button number 2 to select this scene?"

Sandy captures the scene. The fourth and final screen activates, and a scene appears showing the sleeping man's point of view of a streaming showerhead as he takes a shower at the fire station.

"Finally, Miguel, it is your turn to freeze an action on a screen."

Miguel captures the scene, and the Dream Master smiles at them to indicate a job well done.

"This completes the first phase of the process. Each person in the group has captured a freeze-framed image on a vertical screen. Mr. Jones, will you please now press button number 3?"

The words "Ready to Receive Transmission" fade from the main screen. The scenes from the vertical screens—the bride, the fire truck, the shower, and the burning house—fade from the vertical screens and converge on the main screen like a video collage. Then they merge into one continuous action. The audience witnesses the final composition: The fire truck with flashing emergency lights travels down the street while the bride runs along the side and then mounts the truck from the rear. She rides with her gown flowing in the breeze. The truck goes through the neighborhood and stops at a house that is partially engulfed in flames and has a beautiful and well-manicured lawn. A fireman emerges from the interior of the truck with a fire hose across his shoulder. The bride jumps down and assists in carrying the hose to the house. They point the spray from the hose toward the burning house. The water sprays at the house, but the fireman and the bride are the only things getting wet from a gentle stream flowing down directly above their heads. The final composition fades off the screen. The Dream Master looks at the group and then turns to the audience to see their reaction to what they have just witnessed. He says nothing for a minute—just smiles.

"What you have just seen are the random thoughts from a sleeping individual that were captured and merged to make one creation of continuous action. The final product is then transmitted to the brain of the sleeping person, which accepts it as simulated reality or what we refer to as a dream. And we know dreams are weird. Now, you will not know the volume of impulses that will be received. In some cases you might want to wait for the next impulse, which might afford a chance for a more pleasant dream. You will receive a wide variety of thought impulses—some pleasant, some tragic, some good, and some very evil. Your job will be to make the best dream possible with whatever you receive … and, yes, your best might even be a nightmare."

The last statement causes a little stir and worry among the audience. They wonder what exactly it is that they are a part of and how such a program is possible. The Dream Master listens a moment to the soft chatter and then turns squarely to the audience and casually raise his index finger toward them.

"I will let you know right now that we are not privileged to know the results. We don't know what effects our work has on the world of the living. We simply work by faith and believe that we have done something good."

"Faith? That works here?" asks Marcus as he looks around the room.

"Well, that's my way of putting it."

"Well, sir, I need your way to work for me. Is there any way to select a particular person for this dream process?"

"No. As far as we know the process is totally random, with the world's population spread throughout thousands of sectors in the dream world. I don't know whether our sector receives impulses from around the world or from a specific geographical area."

Marcus stares hard and long at the screen. He feels he is possibly at the controls of his brother's war nightmares. He wonders if the Dream Master is telling him the truth or he doesn't really know and is discouraging him from delving into the unknown. Marcus realizes that he must first fully understand his own status. He doesn't know what is next for him and what the expectations are. As he looks around at the others, he asks himself, *Who am I to inquire about these things?* He considers that post-traumatic stress disorder has affected people worldwide. There might be many among the dream makers who have loved ones in the world of the living who are suffering from the disease. He ponders whether he should question the Dream Master further or just be patient. The reality that such a world exists after death is hard for him to comprehend. It is also hard for him to understand his selection to be a dream maker. During life he was aware of lives that seemed to have had specific or even divine purposes, and he wonders if the same applies even now. As the Dream Master explains to the audience the process of dispersing into groups, Marcus raises his finger once again to get his attention.

"How do you choose your dream makers?"

"The tunnel. Remember the twinkling lights in the tunnel? Those are not just decorations but are sensors that record data about those who travel through it. You were scanned and chosen in the tunnel."

"Chosen? Why?" asks Marcus.

Marcus perceives the Dream Master's frustration with his questions. It appears he is not accustomed to a new arrival exhibiting so much curiosity during the orientation phase. He answers with a brisk few words.

"I don't really know. I don't know, and I don't ask. Now it is time for the four of you to go to your theater and get to work. You can go down a corridor and select a vacant theater and perform as you did here. You will be on your own as I prepare the other groups."

Marcus and his group follow the Dream Master to the front foyer where they each arrived. As the group begins to walk in the direction of the corridors, Marcus stops and remains motionless for a moment. He turns to the Dream Master, who anticipates another question.

"Is there something wrong, Mr. Jones?"

Marcus raises his chest slightly. "Well, Mr. Master, I was in law school before, uh, I died, and aren't there some details that need to be discussed before we begin working?"

"What kind of details?"

"Like benefits, wages, rights, and … you know … breaks, lunch, et cetera."

"You are dead, Mr. Jones."

"Okay, but when do we stop for shift changes or to go to our homes?"

"You are dead, Mr. Jones."

Marcus takes a deep breath and surveys his clothes. "So we don't need any of that. What about sleep? Do we sleep?"

"You are dead, Mr. Jones. When you feel sleepy, please let me know and we will talk about it then. I think your group is waiting on you."

CHAPTER 4

Meanwhile, at 4202 Castle Drive in the world of the living, Jacob and Melissa are greeted by Mrs. Jones as they enter through the front door after returning from Jacob's doctor's appointment. As Jacob retreats to the bedroom, Mrs. Jones notices right away that Melissa's appearance today is not her normal well-manicured one from top to bottom. Her hair has a few misplaced strands, and her clothes are slightly soiled. Mrs. Jones also notices a small scratch on Melissa's forehead just below the hairline. Mrs. Jones is deeply concerned about what she sees because she knows that after volunteering to replace Marcus as Jacob's transportation to his appointments, Melissa has always taken him to his appointments and immediately back home.

"Are you all right, dear?" Mrs. Jones asks.

The question causes Melissa to glance down at herself and realize that she has not brushed her clothes sufficiently to remove all the dirt, and, since Mrs. Jones's eyes have also glanced above eye level, she realizes her hair is possibly a little frayed. Melissa brushes her clothes and runs her hands across her hair.

"I'm fine, Mrs. Jones. Really, I am."

Melissa motions for her to come to the kitchen table. Once seated she recounts what happened prior to their arrival to the house:

"Jacob's last appointment was with the psychiatrist. When we left, he was really dejected because the doctor gave him some psychotropic meds for depression, which he claims he doesn't have. Jacob considers the medication to indicate a professional diagnosis that he is mentally ill. I told him the meds were probably just temporary, but that didn't change his feelings. He didn't want to hear that. Well, we left and I decided to stop by the drugstore to buy his meds so you wouldn't have to worry about that. I went into the store alone, and Jacob stayed in the car … or so I thought. When I came out, Jacob was gone. I walked down the sidewalk and saw him making his way through the woods to an area that looked like a camp for the homeless. I called him, but he ignored me. I couldn't see how to get around to him, so I followed his path through the woods—through the brush, tree limbs, leaves, and whatever. When I caught up with him, he was lying on the ground on his back with his hands folded behind his head. I was thinking hard about what to do. I knew I couldn't just leave. So I lay down on my back beside him and folded my hands behind my head."

"My Lord," says Mrs. Jones.

"Then he asked, 'What are you doing?'"

"And I asked him, 'What are you doing?'"

"That's right," says Mrs. Jones.

"Then he told me to go on home and leave him there. He said he didn't want to be anybody's burden anymore. Then he said something that hurt my heart. He said he knew how to survive out there … and if not, dust to dust."

"Oh, really! That's depression talking."

"Yes, ma'am. Then he tried to convince me to leave, because people would think I'm not in my right mind. I told him I was in my right mind, just as he was in his right mind."

"That's correct. He has a wonderful mind."

"Well, I thought about you and got a little upset. I told him that anyone who has a loving mother who is more than willing to help him might not be in his right mind. He didn't say anything else for a while. Then I guess he tried to make me feel better by telling me he knew the guys in the woods and they were just like him—hopeless. Oh, Mrs. Jones, I got angry. I could have used some of those psych meds myself. I screamed, 'What are you talking about, Jacob—war casualties, the walking dead?' I said, 'I thought you went to war to defeat the enemy. The war is not over for you! The ones that set the bomb that killed Macie are also now killing you. They killed your buddies in their land, and they are slowly killing you and others way over here in America.' I said, 'They fought to defeat your ability to survive over there, and now they get double benefit when they defeat your ability to survive here at home. You are still in combat.' Then I said, 'They don't even have to set another bomb, because you have bombs exploding within you.'"

"That is so true."

"Then I said, 'You have to find and destroy those bombs now, and that takes the same amount of training and skill and patience.'"

"That was good."

"Well, he went silent again with his eyes closed. I just looked up through the trees and said, 'Oh, my God. What did I do?' I was afraid that I said too much and talked too much like a family member—like I was his sister or something.'"

"You have been more than a sister. How many people do you know who will spend the time you do with a disabled veteran?"

"Well, then I saw two men walking toward us through the woods, and I got a little scared. I told him about them, but he said nothing. I think he was determined to force me to leave. I lay there and began to think about the army. I think you know that I spent one tour of duty in the army before I went back to school. I was a horrible soldier, but I made it through because the team I was with would not let me quit. I remember being in an obstacle course team competition and being literally dragged through the mud and across the finish line by teammates so we could finish as a team. I thought to myself that we are all a team here fighting this crazy PTSD stuff and we can't quit. I said to myself, *I need to be willing to drag him through the mud if necessary.* Then I felt some liquid run down the side of my face, and I said, 'Oh Lord, is it starting to rain?' I said to myself that this has to stop now. I am going to your house with Jacob. So—forgive me when I say this—but I popped him really hard on the chest with my hand and said 'Get up!'"

"Oh my."

"Then I grabbed his camouflage shirt and pulled him up, and he sat up and looked at me in shock. Mrs. Jones, I was crying and frowning, and I know I looked scary. But

I was serious! I started standing up and wouldn't let go of his shirt as he tried to stand. I put my arms around him and helped him up, and we walked slowly back to the car. He pushed the tree limbs out of my way that time. We made it back to the car okay, and when Jacob entered to sit down, he picked up the meds from the seat and placed them between his legs and just stared at them. I said, 'Buckle up.' He fastened his seat belt while he was staring at the meds. I took off quickly and hoped he wouldn't ask to stop anywhere. As we were going, he finally said something. He said, 'I promised Mom I would pick some vegetables out of her garden.' I said, 'Yes, you did.' I felt myself smiling even though I was still a little upset."

"Now I understand why Ms. Perfection was not so perfect today. And that liquid you felt on your face is your blood."

"Oh, the tree limbs."

Melissa goes to the bathroom to clean her scratch and to freshen up, and for the first time she sees the improvements that were made for Jacob with Marcus's help. She closes the door and leans her back against it and weeps. Meanwhile, Mrs. Jones goes to Jacob's bedroom, where he is on his back on the bed with his eyes closed and his hands folded behind his head. Mrs. Jones slowly sits on the bed beside him, and he raises his head slightly to look at her. He lays his head back on the pillow. Mrs. Jones casually lies on her back beside him and folds her hands behind her head. Jacob looks at her and places his head again on the pillow.

"Someone has been talking," he says.

"Not more than usual. You know how Melissa is."

"Yeah. I'm not surprised."

"I know the doctor gave you some new medicine, so don't forget to take it. It is supposed to help you sleep."

"It might help me sleep, but will it stop the nightmares? I would rather have medicine that keeps me awake."

"But you have to get some decent sleep sometime."

"If I could get just one good peaceful night, I believe I can make it. I'm trying hard, Mom, but I don't know what more I can do. I try to clear my thoughts sometimes, and other times I try to flood my mind with all kinds of thoughts, but none of those changes anything."

"Maybe some good old-fashioned farmwork will help— like plucking corn from the garden."

"Oh yeah. I forgot to do that. I will do it now before it gets dark."

Jacob proceeds to the garden as Melissa emerges from the bathroom. Mrs. Jones watches Jacob from the kitchen window. Melissa joins her as Jacob gets a basket for the vegetables. Jacob is wearing the camouflage shirt and pants that he wears daily.

"I think I understand the camouflage clothing," says Mrs. Jones.

"Yes, they have a purpose," says Melissa.

"His clothes blend with the cornstalks. See that?"

"Yes, I do."

"I just wonder if he will ever blend in again with society and be my Jacob."

"It's going to take time … and miracles still happen."

CHAPTER 5

In the dream world, Marcus and his group finish surveying the corridors and have made a final selection to explore. As they walk toward the corridor, Miguel, a former self-employed tax preparer who was killed during a burglary at his home, makes an observation that he shares with the others.

""Don't you think it strange for there to be an empty theater when you think about all the people who have died and all the people who are living who need dreams?"

"What do you mean?" asks Marcus.

"Well, something must have happened to them, or they would still be here."

"Yeah. Right. Hmm," says Marcus.

Mary crosses her arms and looks at both of them. "I think we should get to work. Maybe there is a penalty for not working. You know, like being fired or something."

"There is always a penalty for not working," says Sandy as she turns toward the corridor. "And since we are dead, I don't want to think of being fired."

The rest think about her statement and turn silently to continue with her down the white marble corridor to choose a theater. They notice several entrances on the right side, each with a set of brown double doors made of engraved wood. Marcus pulls open the first set of doors very slowly. They can see immediately that the theater is occupied and there is activity on the screens. They proceed to the second theater, and as Marcus slowly pulls open the doors, they discover that it is also occupied. As they approach the third theater, they can hear the chatter of others from the orientation room who are now also approaching the same corridor. Marcus slowly opens the doors to the third theater and finds it empty. Marcus pulls the doors wider to reveal the entire room. The group enters upon the white marble floors, which match the color and texture of the marble in the hallway. The room has no windows, and the white walls are bordered at the top and at the bottom with solid wood molding that matches the stain of the doors. They survey a smaller version of the orientation room. There is one horizontal row of five theater chairs that are spaced slightly apart and face a platform of stained wood at the front. Above the platform are a large white screen like the one in the orientation room and four small screens in a vertical row on one side. On the main screen are the words "Ready to Receive Transmission." The members of the group choose their seats and stare at the screen; then they look briefly at one another.

Mary breaks the silence. "Well, here we are."

"Let's get to work. Time is money," says Sandy, a former business consultant who was killed in a plane crash.

"You really don't think we will be paid, do you? We're dead," says Mary.

"There is always a reward for work," says Sandy.

"Do we get credit for quality or weirdness?" asks Miguel.

"All dreams are weird. At least mine are," says Marcus, laughing.

Sandy raises her hand toward the screen and presses button number 1 on her control pad. The words "Ready to Receive Transmission" fade away. A skier who is maneuvering around trees on a downhill run on a snow-covered mountain appears on the screen. The skier comes to the end of a slope and faces an unexpected drop that sends him into a free fall down the slope. Marcus immediately isolates the scene, to Mary's surprise.

"Why did you choose such a tragedy?" asks Mary.

"It's dramatic. We are making miniature movies, and all movies need some action."

"No, Marcus. We are making dreams people have to live with. They need pleasant dreams."

"Right. Like my brother."

Marcus watches as the scene of the skier is followed on the next screen by a white SUV that rolls into the driveway of a house where a young couple and two children are standing on the porch. The children run to the SUV playfully and enter a side door.

"This one is mine," says Mary. "Any thoughts of children at play make for a pleasant dream."

The scene of children is followed by a scene of a tavern with men at the bar in conversation and laughter. Sandy chooses the tavern scene. On the fourth screen are the images of a doctor and a medical team who rush a bed down a hallway of a hospital. They walk toward the sleeping person in his point of view. Miguel chooses the scene of the hospital.

"Well," says Miguel, "it looks like the men chose the tragedies and the women the pleasantries."

"Well, let's finish it up and see who wins," says Sandy. "I wonder if we are being timed."

"You think so?" asks Mary.

"Like I said before—I don't want to think of being fired. The primary reason for most firings is poor performance."

She presses button number 3 to transfer the scenes to the main screen for the merger. The final composition shows the skier digging frantically with his poles to avoid trees and stay on balance before the free fall. He suddenly sees himself traveling down the slope in a chairlift to the double doors at the entrance of a tavern. Two kids open the doors as a doctor and a medical team appear with a bed with an IV attached and approach him. He is carried briskly down a hallway of a hospital to an operating room. The group look at one another with a sign of approval and transmit the composition as a dream.

"That was really weird," says Marcus, "but not bad."

"Weird but not bad for our first production," agrees Miguel.

"Yes," says Mary. "The skiing accident was diluted by thoughts of other things. Weird, but I like it."

"We're on a roll," says Marcus as he points his control at the screen to receive brain impulses from another sleeper.

There appear three men engaged in a meeting in a small conference room. One of them speaks the name "Ritchie" while passing money across the table. Sandy captures the scene as it begins to fade. On the second small screen are two men in jackets who are walking to the rear of a café at night. They confront a well-dressed man in a suit who has just approached his car. One of the two men pulls out a gun from under his jacket and shouts out the name "Ritchie." The well-dressed man turns and is shot three times. He collapses to the ground while the two men hurry away. Marcus isolates the scene as he leans forward to stare at it for a moment.

"What do have we here—a murder?" he asks.

"It sure looks like it," says Sandy. "And we are witnesses."

"Postmortem," adds Mary.

After staring intently at the screen, Marcus rises and proceeds quickly to the exit. As he pushes the doors open, Miguel calls out to him, "Where are you going?"

"I'll be back. We have to report this."

Marcus jogs down the hallway to the orientation room, where the Dream Master is making a presentation to a new group of arrivals. The Dream Master pauses as he hears footsteps and then sees Marcus suddenly at the door. The Dream Master walks briskly to him.

"What is it, Marcus?"

"I believe we are witnesses to a murder. Someone has thoughts of shooting a man in cold blood."

The Dream Master takes a big sigh of relief. "You will see many things, and some of them will be really gruesome and downright evil. Your job is to make a dream of whatever you see on the screens."

"Being a law student, I felt an obligation to say something. Plus, I remember a movie named *Ghost* with Whoopi

Goldberg and Patrick Swayze where they were able to do something with their mind and body that sent a message to the living. They did some kind of 'umph' by pushing out their chests."

The Dream Master laughs and places his right hand on Marcus's left shoulder. He says softly, "They were acting, but you are really dead, Mr. Jones."

"Not possible, huh?"

"No. And I believe your group is waiting for you."

Marcus lowers his head and walks swiftly back to his theater, where the rest of the group anxiously await the outcome of his discussion. As Marcus enters, all eyes turn toward him, but he walks directly to his seat and slumps down without speaking.

"What is the verdict?" asks Sandy.

"There is nothing we can do. We might see some gruesome things, but there is nothing we can do about them."

Miguel taps his chin with his index finger and states, "Let's see. Is that because we are dead, Mr. Jones?"

"You got that right."

CHAPTER 6

In the world of the living, a memorial service is in progress for Marcus Jones in the chapel of a local funeral home. Marcus's remains are in a stone-gray casket with brass corner ornaments and rails. Melissa admires the beauty of the casket as it rests open at the front of the chapel. It is a few feet from the first row, where she sits with Mrs. Jones, Jacob, and a few other relatives. Melissa, though very saddened, feels some solace in seeing the many stunned and tearful friends of Marcus who have just finished viewing the body. She grabs Mrs. Jones's hand as the funeral staff's attention turns to the family for their viewing. She escorts a very tearful Mrs. Jones to the casket as members of the funeral home staff walk on either side of them. As she slowly approaches the casket, Mrs. Jones grips the side with her right hand as she bends over and reaches out with her left hand to touch Marcus's forehead. Melissa watches closely as she moves her hand gently down the tie and the jacket until her hand reaches his hands, which are resting one on the other at his waist. She grasps his hands and whispers, "I miss you, son. I miss you."

She turns to Melissa to indicate that she is ready to return to her seat. Melissa escorts her to her seat and watches the funeral staff escort Jacob to the front. She leans forward as Jacob reaches out with both hands to brace himself slightly on the casket. She can tell that through the grief and physical discomfort from his back injury Jacob struggles to maintain an erect posture in his army ceremonial uniform. For once he has replaced the daily army jungle fatigues with a different set of clothes. He lowers his head and speaks quietly to himself.

"I wish I could have been there for you."

Melissa stares at him with grave concern and nervously anticipates the need to rush to the casket to assist him. As she watches him, she visualizes him as an active-duty soldier. She agonizes over the thought of his bearing the burden of the death of his best army friend and now the death of his only brother, who was his primary source of strength at home. She wonders how there can be an effective program of rehabilitation for soldiers with PTSD caused by military experience when civilian life adds its own set of tragedies. She lowers her head in conclusion that a miracle might be the only answer. Jacob lowers his head to the edge of the casket momentarily, and the funeral staff move closer to him. Melissa stands, but Jacob raises his head and motions that he is all right and returns to his seat. After all the immediate family and relatives have viewed the remains, the minister approaches the podium and motions for the casket to be closed. As the lid is slowly closed, Melissa notices the sweat that is forming on Jacob's forehead. She first attributes the sweat to the uniform, especially the tie, which he is not accustomed to wearing. She also notices that he is either taking deep and prolonged breaths or is having breathing difficulty. It seems to her that he is struggling to hold back an outburst of grief. Melissa rises and sits between Jacob and Mrs. Jones. She clutches his hands with a firm grip.

"Is Jacob all right?" asks Mrs. Jones.

"Yes, ma'am. He is going to be just fine."

She maintains a firm grip throughout the rest of the ceremony. At the end of the memorial she releases his hand as the family is asked to stand for the processional out of the chapel. She dabs the sweat from his forehead with a tissue, and he turns to her.

"I wish I could have been there for him."

"I know, Jacob, and he knows too."

"We all wish the same," says Mrs. Jones as they follow behind the casket.

Later that day at 4202 Castle Drive, Mrs. Jones opens the door for paramedics who have just arrived outside in response to her call for emergency assistance for Jacob. She returns to cradle him on the floor, where he is holding his chest and grimacing in pain. Her embrace and words of consolation are ineffective at the present. She watches as the paramedics enter and provide treatment for a preliminary diagnosis of abnormal cardiac rhythm and prepare him for transport. Mrs. Jones gathers her jacket and purse and follows them out the door. She texts a brief message to Melissa before leaving the driveway. While sitting in her car she can see a neighbor standing across the street and looking in her direction. She exits the driveway and speeds past another neighbor and his kids, who have apparently stopped their play to observe the activity at the Joneses' house. When Mrs. Jones arrives at the hospital and begins to walk through the parking lot, she sees Melissa standing at the emergency room entrance.

"I got your text."

"It's Jacob. I think he is having a heart attack," says Mrs. Jones as they walk swiftly to the emergency room.

"I was worried about him at the funeral."

"I am at a loss for words right now. Not Jacob too."

"This is a trauma center, so I'm sure he is getting the best."

"But why do I have to come here again? Why, Lord?"

When they enter the reception area, Melissa steps forward to identify herself and Mrs. Jones, and inquires about Jacob. They are informed that Jacob has been quickly stabilized and is now undergoing a series of tests and monitoring. They are directed to the waiting area.

"What am I going to do?" asks Mrs. Jones.

"We're going to get through this—you, Jacob, and me. Let's see what the doctor says."

"You took care of Marcus and Jacob, and now you are going to take care of me too. I told Marcus jokingly that I thought you were an angel. Maybe it wasn't a joke after all."

"I'm no angel. Marcus could have told you that … and Jacob, since he has my handprints on his chest."

"Angels have to do what they have to do, dear."

They see two white full-length automatic doors open as a doctor emerges. He calls for Mrs. Jones and motions for her to join him. Melissa follows and notices that the doctor is greeting them with a smile.

"Mr. Jones is doing fairly well right now, but he has some major complications that need to be cleared up. I have been in contact with his cardiologist at the VA hospital. That's Dr. Milfred Rodriguez. Based on our test results he is coming here to consider open-heart surgery."

"Jacob is not going to be transferred to the VA hospital?" asks Mrs. Jones.

"No. That's not necessary anymore. New laws allow him to receive follow-up treatment here from his doctor. Dr. Rodriguez is a former combat medic, and he happens to know Jacob very well. He will take good care of him."

"Yes. We know him well. I need my son."

CHAPTER 7

In the dream world Marcus stands and moves closer to one of the small screens to stare at what appears to be weapons fire and explosions. He begins to see soldiers emerging from the smoke who are scurrying into an abandoned building while engaged in a firefight. Marcus continues to stare as the scene fades. He waits for a different type of transmission, but the scene is followed by more active combat.

"Marcus, you have to select one so we can move on," says Mary.

Marcus selects the most recent combat scene. He watches as the second screen activates and also shows a scene of field combat, and more scenes are displayed on the third and fourth screens. When he realizes that scenes of combat have been selected by all members of the group, he walks back and forth in front of the screens with his head down.

"We can't do this!" he says.

"Do what?" Mary asks.

"We can't send this man or this woman a dream composed totally of combat."

"If he or she is on the battlefield, then the dominant thoughts will be of war."

"Yes, he might be on actual combat duty," says Sandy.

"Or he or she might be a veteran fighting with the plague of PTSD like my brother. I don't want to perpetuate that plague."

Miguel asks, "But what are we supposed to do? The Dream Master told you we will see many things and we are to ignore them and do our job. Plus, how are we to know what's going on in the world of the living?"

Miguel folds his arms as he watches Marcus sit and lean forward on one arm of his chair. Suddenly and to everyone's surprise, Marcus rushes out of the theater. Marcus jogs to the foyer and sees the Dream Master walking down a corridor.

"Mr. Master!"

The Dream Master is startled and turns to see Marcus jogging toward him. Marcus speaks before he can ask a question.

"Excuse me, sir. I know it is unusual for someone to question you about what goes on here, but I have a brother in the world of the living who is suffering with nightmares of war. I wish there was some way we could give him just one good night of rest."

"He has what is called in your time post-traumatic stress disorder?"

"Yeah! You know about that?"

"We know about that. What your era calls military post-traumatic stress has been in the world since the beginning of warfare. In fact, since you obviously can't keep to task, let me show you some things from my archive of dream impulses from another era. I believe you will find them quite interesting."

Marcus follows the Dream Master into the main theater where the orientations are held. The room is empty. The Dream Master manipulates some controls on the gadget in his hand, which is more complex than the ones dream makers use. The word *war* appears on the screen followed by the word *soldier* and *Roman* and then *battle*. Several flashes of active ancient combat appear on the screen. The Dream Master freezes an image of a soldier standing arrayed in his battle armor and brandishing a sword.

"These are thoughts from an ancient soldier. You see him with his sword drawn and preparing for a one-on-one battle."

Another image appears on the screen. It is the still image of a full-body close-up of a charging enemy soldier with his sword drawn. Marcus sits quietly as the scenes are put into motion and the soldiers engage in a sword fight on the battlefield. The images of flailing swords and shields dominate the screen. The Dream Master freezes the frame.

"Consider this man's thoughts. He heard the footsteps of the charging enemy. He saw the anger on his face and heard the growling and cursing from his lips. Upon each stroke of the sword he felt the strength of his enemy's body while the clashing of swords and shields rang in his ears. And he heard the numerous shouts and moans of other combatants on the battlefield. Those were his thoughts when he lay down to sleep … and there is this."

Marcus watches as the images on the screen change to a bloody hand piercing the torso of a soldier and withdrawing the sword in a gush of blood.

"This soldier had a thought of his hand thrusting a sword into a man's belly and feeling his warm blood run down his hands and arms. The battle might have just begun, which means he might have had to pierce many more men with the same sword and also feel their blood run down his arm. Blood was constantly upon him—his face, his clothes—as he walked through the field of slain bodies in the continuous battle."

Marcus watches as the screen shows the soldier kneeling by a stream and removing his tools of war after the battle. The screen then shows a hand being gradually submerged into one large red ripple that covers the screen.

"After the battle he found water to wash himself and his sword and sheath. He watched the blood radiate through the water and ripple back and forth as he washed. See how he sometimes let his hands linger in the bloody water? What level of post-traumatic stress do you think he had when he lay down to sleep? How did he feel when he sat down later with his family to eat after being splattered for days with the blood of combat? He might have had the same imaginary thoughts as the wife of Macbeth, who cried, 'Out, damned spot!' She was plagued psychologically by her thoughts of imaginary blood on her hands, but the soldier's thoughts were based on actual deeds."

The scene is switched again. A woman, a child, and the soldier sit at a wooden table that is prepared with vessels containing food and drink. While in conversation with the woman, the soldier lifts a cup of drink partially to his lips and then slams the cup to the table. The drink spills across the table. He then tosses the cup to the floor. The woman stands and grabs the child while backing away from the table. The soldier rakes some of the food vessels off the table as the child cringes in fear. He stands and shouts, "I can't help it. This is what I am!" as he rips open his top garment to reveal his many scars from battle. He then grabs his sword and sheath from the wall and stumbles out.

"Yes, Mr. Jones. Post-traumatic stress disorder has been with humanity a long time."

"I've never thought about it as part of ancient history. Wow! That's interesting!"

"It's all throughout history. The soldiers struggled with the requirements of being a soldier, a citizen, and head of a family. The really sad part of that era is that the soldier was never retired from war and was always in possession of his weapon. He was used by the government to protect the country and also to keep the domestic peace. Because of the constant pressure from continual conflict, many fell on their swords and others went back to the battlefield to die."

Marcus analyzes intently what he sees on the screen and wonders what else the system can do. While the Dream Master speaks, Marcus takes another opportunity to speak of his obsession with the possibility of individual selection in the dream-making process.

"Was there nothing you could do here?"

"No. We can only make their dreams less traumatic if we receive the right kind of thought impulses."

"You say there is no way to select a particular individual for a dream composition?"

"That's correct."

"There is absolutely nothing that can be converted or rigged to bypass the system? You know, like you can't hack into any cyberspace anywhere? There are no secret dream world files anywhere with everyone's personal information that can mysteriously pop up on your system here?"

The Dream Master snaps back and points in the direction of the foyer. "As I indicated earlier, the only identifier is the tunnel. The person would have to be deceased and passing through the tunnel's scanning process. That is the only way. And again, I believe your group is missing you."

"Yes, sir," says Marcus, as he fears that the Dream Master's frustration has turned into anger.

Marcus turns and walks slowly to his theater. The Dream Master takes a deep breath and turns to stare at the screen. He places his hands on his hips and looks in Marcus's direction. He lowers his head and then takes another deep breath.

CHAPTER 8

In the world of the living, Jacob awakes and stares at the blank screen on the TV as he lies in bed in the hospital. He tries to ignore the two IV bags and the heart monitor to his left that are connected to him and are constant reminders that he is scheduled for heart surgery today. He sits up on the bed to look around the room for the TV remote but is unable to locate it. He returns to a prone position on the bed and stares at the spikes on the silent heart monitor. He hears a nurse outside the door and smiles when she enters the room to check the monitor and IV setup.

"Do you have the TV remote?" he asks.

"No, I don't. We need you to just rest right now. We will be in soon to prep you for surgery."

"You want me to rest by looking at dancing spikes on the monitor and the slow drips in the IV tubes?"

"Okay. I'm going to let you look at TV until we hear from the doctor. He should be here soon."

"Thanks. You're the best nurse ever."

"Then I'm going to take it from you."

She looks around the room and finds the TV remote on the windowsill beside the adjacent bed and gives it to him as she leaves. He flips through the channels and stops at a news station when he sees the words "Continued War in the Middle East" displayed behind the commentator. He increases the volume and places a pillow under his shoulder to raise his head. He listens intently to the commentator:

"Two more soldiers were killed yesterday in Afghanistan after their vehicle ran over a land mine in the undeclared war in the Middle East. The numbers of deaths and injuries creep upward daily. Speaking of war deaths—the traveling replica of the Vietnam War Memorial has arrived in Spokane, Washington, as you see here, so the people can pay tribute and scratch on paper the names of their loved ones, friends, and war comrades who died in the Vietnam War. As we watch this we can't help but ask who is designing a memorial for the war casualties of the Middle East, for those two soldiers killed yesterday, and the others.

"In the local news the police are searching for the gunman who shot and killed a store clerk in last night's convenience store robbery. The police have released this video of the shooting, which shows the suspect shooting the clerk point-blank after receiving the cash. The police have released this sketch of the suspect wearing a black hood. They believe he is responsible for the latest rash of robberies in the county. The police need your help in finding this guy."

Jacob turns his head from the TV and stares again at the heart monitor. He drops the TV remote as he sees a changing pattern on the heart monitor and feels a tightening in his chest along with gradually increasing pain. He presses the call button at his bed.

"Yes, Mr. Jones?"

"I need a nurse."

Jacob sees two nurses enter the room. One approaches him as the other checks the display on the monitor.

"What's wrong, Mr. Jones?"

"I'm having chest pain."

"We need to move him to the ICU," says the other nurse.

The nurse at the bedside leaves as the other nurse secures the cords and IV lines. The nurse returns with additional help, and Jacob is transported down the hall to the intensive care unit for further monitoring. As he is rolled down the hall, Jacob can hear "Dr. Rodriguez to ICU. Dr. Rodriguez to ICU." ring out from the intercoms along the hallways. While he is entering the ICU, Jacob gasps for breath and faintly sees a nurse strap an oxygen mask to his face. Jacob loses consciousness, and the heart monitor registers a flat line. Dr. Rodriguez enters as a nurse reaches over Jacob with defibrillator paddles to administer a shock to his chest. Dr. Rodriguez sees that the shock registers no spike on the heart monitor. He takes the paddles and administers another shock, which nets the same result. He asks for increased voltage and applies the paddles six more times, producing a violent arching of Jacob's body each time. He stares at the persistent flat line with noticeably heightened frustration and then lowers his head. He looks at the nurses and nods to prompt them to begin the normal follow-up protocol. He steps away slowly to retrieve his iPad to record the event and the time of Jacob's death.

"Good-bye, friend," he whispers.

As he begins to walk toward the door, he thinks of the unpleasant task of informing another family that a loved one has died … and in this case, the loved one and the family are his friends. He is truly concerned about the impact on Mrs. Jones, who has lost both her sons in a short time span. He lingers at the door and looks back and stares at the body.

He is unaware that Jacob has begun his journey through the same proverbial tunnel as Marcus did to the light. Jacob enters awestricken by the sparkling data collectors that enshroud him. The information gathered about him causes the Dream Master to rush down the hall to his operation room to respond to the beeping sound of a notification alert. As he deactivates the alarm, he notices that the alert is in response to his request that a copy of data files on any soldier named Jacob Jones be forwarded to Sector 10247. He discovered after Marcus's persistent questioning that the tunnel process can't be changed, but a copy of the individual profiles are available upon request before an individual is channeled to a final destination. He is excited because he knows that the individual might be Marcus's brother.

"Jacob Jones!"

But his excitement is quickly tempered by the realization that if it is Marcus's brother, then he has to inform him that his brother has died.

Meanwhile, back in the world of the living, Dr. Rodriguez places his hand on the handle of the door that leads from the room to the hallway. As his hand grips the handle, he places his forehead against the door and then turns to look at Jacob's body, which has now been covered with a white cloth. He thinks about this highly trained and dedicated military man who would not quit the fight for his country. He knows that Jacob would be on the battlefield right now if he was allowed to and was able. Dr. Rodriguez asks himself, *Is this a fitting end for a fighter?* He snaps around to the team, who are slowly replacing the equipment.

"Everyone! One more time! One more time! Quick!"

The bewildered team scurry to prepare Jacob and the equipment as Dr. Rodriguez prepares his hands to receive the defibrillator paddles. He orders a higher voltage than the last administered shock. He applies the paddles, and the shock causes Jacob's body to arch violently upward, but he sees no positive result on the heart monitor. He applies the paddles again with obvious deep frustration, but the result is the same—Jacob's heart is nonresponsive. He glances at the worried eyes of the staff as he prepares to administer a third shock. As he applies the paddles, he screams, "Jacob!"

Miraculously, a spike appears. One spike travels alone across the screen before the starring and unbelieving eyes of everyone. Before the single spike exits the screen, a series of spikes appear and begin a trek across the screen. Dr. Rodriguez watches the spikes travel consistently for several minutes as the IV is reattached to Jacob's arm.

"Notify the hospital that surgery will be performed today as scheduled. Take him to the operating room. I am going now to scrub, but first, where is my iPad? He's alive."

A nurse hands him the iPad with a smile.

Back in the dream world Jacob has stopped moving forward in the tunnel. All lights are quickly extinguished as the tunnel shuts down.

What's happening? the Dream Master asks himself. *That's it? I didn't get a complete file.*

He checks the controls and discovers there has been an abrupt termination of the data stream, which means there is no longer a person in the tunnel. He wonders if he received enough information in the queue to positively identify the individual. He transfers the data to a program that converts it to a visual format. He watches closely as a visual presentation begins on the screen. He fast-forwards the data for a speedier review. He notices that the information appears to be an age progression of the individual. He begins to search for the young adult life when a young man would enlist in the army, but the data terminates during the preadolescent ages. He sulks in his chair as he realizes there is not enough information to determine if this individual is a soldier and also no way to determine his relationship, if any, to Marcus. He reverses the presentation to take a more deliberate scan of some of the people in this individual's life. He stops on a frame showing a young boy standing alone on pavement with a small American flag that he waves over his head. He notices that the young boy is dressed in a camouflage vest and green pants. He magnifies the image and is amazed.

"Marcus! Is that you?"

He is almost convinced that he is looking at a young Marcus Jones. He hurries away from the screen and walks swiftly down the corridor to the theater where Marcus and his group are working. He opens a door slowly, leans in, and immediately gets the group's attention. He points to Marcus and motions for him to come to the door. As Marcus approaches, the Dream Master says nothing and walks away swiftly down the corridor to his work area, with Marcus following closely behind.

"There is something very interesting that I want you to see."

"That's me!" shouts Marcus immediately as he approaches closer to the screen.

"Are you sure?"

"Yes! I was wearing the imitation flak jacket that Jacob made for me. He sewed foil paper to the inside of the vest for my imaginary protection when we played war games. He handed me a small American flag before leaving for his second tour of duty. I asked him why he had to go back to the army. He said, 'For America, for you, and for the flag.' How did you get this picture?"

"It was in a partial transmission from the tunnel. I requested a copy of any data on soldiers named Jacob Jones be forwarded to our sector."

Marcus stares silently at the screen and then turns slowly and stares at the Dream Master, who has turned slightly away from him.

"From the tunnel?"

"Yes."

"That means Jacob is dead, doesn't it?"

"Normally, yes. However, I didn't receive a complete file, and I don't know why. This has happened before, but it is extremely rare. It has happened a few times when someone has been brought back to life after entering the tunnel."

Marcus places his hands on top of his head. "So you are saying it is possible that Jacob died and was revived?"

"That's a stretch and a possibility."

"Now what? How can we know? What can we do?" asks Marcus as he turns to look at the screen again, which still displays his magnified image.

"Whoa! Remember this is the afterlife. Any attempt to communicate with the living is strictly forbidden. However, this is so fascinating that even though I don't want to tread on the forbidden, I would love to explore the limits."

He stands and then paces and ponders for a moment; then he sits down again and begins to do a verbal analysis of what has been happening to determine if there is any possibility of manipulating the system.

"Let's see—we can receive data from the tunnel in all sectors, but we have never sent data through the tunnel in the opposite direction as a tracer of sorts. I am wondering if we now have a traceable path back to a specific individual. That's the question you have been asking, sort of. Of course the person will have to be sleeping for a dream composition, and we have no way of determining whether he is."

"Let's do this!"

"Patience. It will not be easy. We will have to move very cautiously step-by-step. The first step is to pray that this is not forbidden."

Marcus blinks both eyes and says, "Done!"

The Dream Master taps on his workstation and again thinks out loud to himself. Marcus sits and taps on his knees in nervous anticipation.

"Okay, the brain impulses that are sent to the theater from the sleepers are temporary data files that are discarded if they aren't used in the dream-making process. But the files that are collected in the tunnel are normally a complete data package in a specific format. The information must come from the tunnel as a complete package. But what if it doesn't? I need to research some system records."

He taps a question into his control, and an answer appears on his screen. He and Marcus take a moment to read the answer.

The file is rejected and then converted to a temporary file folder in the system. It will remain there as an inactive personnel file until data are received again from the person to whom it belongs. Whenever new data are received from that person, the inactive folder is activated.

"The question now is whether the data from death processing can be used in dream processing. If so, the information from the tunnel might be incorporated into the dream-making process when that individual sleeps."

"You are saying that since this file is from Jacob, then when he sleeps his brain impulses might be transferred here to match the information you have?"

"Correct, I believe."

"I believe it, too."

CHAPTER 9

In the world of the living, Mrs. Jones holds Jacob's hands as he gradually awakens in the ICU after undergoing open-heart surgery. She positions his pillow so his head is slightly elevated. He slowly looks down at himself and notices the straps around his body and the protective railings on both sides of the bed. He turns to look at the nurse who has just come in to check the heart monitor and IV connections. She is followed very shortly by Dr. Rodriguez and Melissa, who is carrying a bedroom-style pillow.

"Are you awake?" asks Dr. Rodriguez. "You did great. We had to do a triple bypass, but there were no complications. You should have a good recovery if you follow orders … I mean instructions."

"You are doing well, and you are going to get much better." says Mrs. Jones.

"It looks like my sleep wasn't so good with these straps."

"Yes," responds Mrs. Jones. "You had some rough moments just like at home, so precautions had to be taken."

"I'm ready to get up."

"Don't worry. We are going to get you home as soon as possible," says Dr. Rodriguez. "But right now you need more rest. You did get a little sleep, and a little sleep is better than no sleep. I know we are dealing with a catch-22. Sleep enhances your recovery, but it's what you see in your sleep that disrupts your ability to really rest. You need more deep sleep."

"Son, if there was ever a time that we need to have a little faith, it is now."

"And we have it. You have it," says Melissa. "You must sleep a little more, and I will be right by your bed when you wake up."

"Thanks. I'm sure that won't be long," he says.

The nurse prepares a syringe after consultation with Dr. Rodriguez and proceeds to inject medication into an IV line. Jacob stares into his mother's eyes as the medication takes effect. Mrs. Jones moves her head slowly up and down as Jacob gradually falls back to sleep.

"He should sleep until morning. Someone will contact you if there are any problems."

"Thank you, sir. Melissa, I'm going home. I will see you in the morning."

"Okay. Get some rest yourself. I will be right here."

Meanwhile in the dream world, the Dream Master hurries once again to his workstation because of a notification he is receiving on his hand control. He checks his system and realizes the forwarded data he is now receiving belong to the previously forwarded files from the tunnel. Those data belong to Jacob Jones. He notices also that the data are in dream format. Since his station does not create dream compositions as do the theaters, he alerts Marcus's group over the intercom to prepare to receive a special transmission. The group hurry to complete the dream composition that is in progress. As the screen resets to receive the information from the Dream Master, Mary, Miguel, and Sandy turn to look at Marcus.

"This is it! This is my brother!"

"How is that possible?" asks Mary.

"I don't know. It has something to do with the tunnel."

Everyone turns to the screen and stares very hard at the screen as the words "Ready to Receive Transmission" fade away. The first vertical screen activates and shows young Marcus standing alone and waving a small American flag. The scene is immediately captured by Marcus.

"That's me!"

Then the Dream Master enters quickly and stands behind the group. He has never had the opportunity to know to whom dream processing information belonged. Now he not only knows to whom it belongs, but he also has a member of his staff closely associated with the person.

"This is amazing! A first!"

Marcus watches closely as the second screen activates and shows soldiers in combat gear scrambling to their vehicles as the "fire in the hole" call is given three times. The call is followed by an explosion that sends dirt and rocks in the direction of the vehicles. No one selects the scene, but to their surprise the scene repeats on the second screen.

"Miguel, please select it so we can move on," says the Dream Master.

"There has got to be something else coming," says Marcus.

"Maybe so, but we must move on with the process. There are two more screens left."

The third screen activates, and everyone sees another scene of soldiers on the battlefield. Two soldiers walk along a dirt road in one of the soldiers' point of view. Marcus can hear the combat boots grinding pebbles as they step and notices that each soldier is operating a metal detector in search of explosives. He watches as one of the soldiers steps across a rock and freezes. He then hears the other soldier yell, "What's up, man?"

"That's my brother, Jacob."

Suddenly a red flash occurs that covers the screen, and burnt fragments of clothing shoot to the center of the screen.

"That's it! That's the bomb!"

Marcus now sees before his eyes the cause of Jacob's torment. He is spellbound and almost moved to tears as he watches the action scene repeat. The group wait impatiently for the scene to change to nonmilitary activities, but then the Dream Master asks Sandy to freeze the scene as a selection. Marcus is speechless as he snaps around to look at the Dream Master.

"We must go on."

"I can't allow this. I can't allow these images to continue to be part of my brother's dreams!"

"That's all we have so far, and we must move on. We still have one more screen."

"One more? One more? How can I expect anything different?"

"Let's just see. We must move on. Let's keep the faith."

"That faith stuff again! Can't you do something please?"

"I'm sorry I can't. Let's move on."

As the fourth screen activates, Marcus can see a small pair of black women's low-cut casual shoes that are walking through a newly planted vegetable garden. The scene widens to show Mrs. Jones placing a plastic covering over the area to prevent the birds and animals from eating the seeds.

"That's Mom! Save it!"

Mary immediately saves the scene, and a little hope returns to the group. Everyone's eyes now focus on the main screen in a moment of silence. Each of them seems to wonder what weird final composition will result. Mary looks at the Dream Master, who nods his head in approval for the process to be finalized. Everyone now looks at Marcus.

"The privilege is yours," says the Dream Master.

"How do we know if that is enough?"

"That's all we have, and we must go on or lose everything."

Meanwhile in the world of the living, Melissa is curled in a chair and covered with a thin white hospital blanket at Jacob's bedside while he sleeps. She notices Jacob's arm rise to the height of the protective railing of the bed and also his head move slowly from side to side. She also notices that his breathing rate seems to have slightly increased. She approaches the bed and grasps his hand firmly with both of hers. She stares at him in anticipation of further movement and a possible need for staff assistance. She pats his hands gently and closes her eyes as she bows her head.

Back in the dream world, Marcus presses button number 3. The scenes from the small screens transfer and merge on the main screen into one continuous action. The final composition shows soldiers with metal detectors walking behind Mrs. Jones in her newly planted garden as she moves forward to spread a plastic cover over the area. Her garden butts against the small pile of stones that hides the land mine. She spreads the covering over both the garden and the stones. The land mine explodes and lifts the covering into a huge plastic mound of fire as the ground shakes all around. Mrs. Jones and the soldiers watch the plastic mound slowly deflate downward as the ground ceases to shake. When the plastic settles to the ground, there is no fire or smoke rising above it. No one is injured. Instead, full-grown stalks of corn push up rapidly through the covering and surround Mrs. Jones and the soldiers. The soldiers in their camouflage combat uniforms pluck ears of corn from the stalks. All the soldiers are soon laden with armfuls of corn, which they place in baskets at Mrs. Jones's feet. Mrs. Jones approaches a soldier whose face is not shown and says, "Thank you, son." As the soldiers continue their search with their detectors, little Marcus can be seen at the edge of the garden smiling and waving his little American flag. The composition fades and is transmitted as a dream for Jacob.

At the same time in the world of the living, Melissa opens her eyes at Jacob's bedside and sees a calming of his breathing and feels the muscles in his hand relax. She jumps back a little with surprise when a snore spurts from his mouth. She smiles as the snoring continues and gradually gets louder and reverberates throughout the unit. The loud and whistling snores attract the attention of the medical staff, and two of them gather around his bed in laughter. At that moment Mrs. Jones is buzzed into the area carrying two cups of coffee on a fast-food drink tray. She can see Melissa and the nurses at Jacob's bed, but can't hear the conversations.

"Oh Lord," she says to herself.

She begins to shake with worry and increases her pace while balancing the fast-food tray. She arrives at Jacob's bed only to hear laughter. She sees everyone's eyes on the opening and closing of his mouth as he whistle-snores. She remembers that Jacob is a snorer, but she has not heard him do so since he returned from the army.

"I haven't heard him do that since he came home from the army," says Mrs. Jones.

"Sounds like he is deep in sleep," says a nurse.

"That's music to me."

The conversations and laughter cause Jacob to stir and awaken, still under partial influence of the sleep medication. He stretches his eyes to see those around him and smiles when he recognizes his mother.

"I want to tell you about my dream," he says, and then he drifts back to sleep and to snoring.

"I guess you will have to tell me about it later."

After two days of recovery at the hospital, Jacob arrives home with Mrs. Jones and Melissa. He pauses a few feet inside the front door and takes a deep breath.

"Now, this smells like home."

"Yes. You're home, son."

"Something's missing."

"What's that?"

"I don't smell anything in the kitchen."

"Well, I can fix that real quick. But of course, it will have to be according to the doctor's orders … I mean instructions."

"Yeah. I guess we'd better read his orders … I mean instructions."

CHAPTER 10

The clock on the nightstand shows three o'clock in the morning as Jacob lies awake in his bed at home.

"Little Marcus!" he says with a smile as he looks to the ceiling.

He slowly rises to a sitting position on the side of the bed and meditates a moment. He notices the small reading light is still on at his writing desk in the corner near the foot of the bed. He approaches the desk and reaches for the lamp but pauses to look once again at the news article and the police report about Marcus's death. The papers have remained at the end of the desk since the incident. He reaches for a book at the other end and moves it closer to the light to study the title once again: *Living with PTSD*. He places the book on top of the papers and turns off the light. He then turns the light back on and slowly walks to the closet at the opposite end and pulls out a green army duffel bag. He moves the bag closer to the light and takes out a pair of black army dress shoes and turns them over to inspect them. He searches in the bag and finds the cleaner, polish, and rags he uses to take care of them. He cleans and polishes them on the desk and then places each shoe between his knees for a brisk rag-popping buff that brings sweat to his brow and a few panting breaths. Then he lifts the pair of shoes in his left hand and wiggles four fingers of his right hand over the shoes to admire the reflection. He puts his fingers together in a pinch and blows on them as he rubs them together.

"I'm still the best."

He replaces the polish and rags into the duffel bag and puts the bag into the closet. He clears a spot on the closet shelf and gently places the shoes there. He returns to bed and turns on his side to sleep some more.

Later in the morning Mrs. Jones, wearing a cooking apron, approaches the door to Jacob's room and listens for any stirring. She knocks on the door, but there is no answer. She knocks again with the same result. She opens the door slowly as she continues to knock gently upon the door. She sees that Jacob is fast asleep. She wishes that he could continue to sleep, but she knows he has an outpatient physical therapy appointment today. She approaches his bed very slowly, which gives him as many additional seconds of sleep as possible. But as she reaches the bed he awakes and sees her standing over him.

"Have you been there long?"

"I just came in a few seconds ago. You were sleeping so well I hated to wake you."

"No problems again."

"That sounds good."

"Maybe it is because everyone in my dream was too busy picking corn for you."

"Picking corn? What do you mean?"

"Well, in the hospital I had this weird dream about you and your garden. There was a crazy explosion and no one got killed, but there was a burst of cornstalks. They were like the song says, "as high as an elephant's eye," and there were big ears too. So I and my army buddies picked corn for you while we searched for bombs."

"Oh, really? That sounds a little strange. I was in the army with you and your army buddies?"

"Mom, you know dreams are weird. But the best part was little Marcus. Little Marcus was standing around waving the little American flag I gave him when he was a little boy."

"Marcus? I see you are mentioning him with a smile. Was he in the army too?"

"No, ma'am. I'm smiling because he was in my dream. I said out loud, "Little Marcus!" He has left the chair again and entered my dreams. I forgot about that flag. He really loved it. I said to him, 'I am going to the army for America, for you, and for the flag.'"

"Then keep telling that to Marcus and to yourself. Then tell yourself that you are also fighting this PTSD stuff for America, for you, and for the flag. The fight is not over, but you're winning!"

"Yes, sir! I don't know what changed my dreams, but after that strange dream I finally got a good night of sleep. It felt good. I believe I am on my way to making it now."

"Well, I know where you are going to spend a lot of time."

"Where's that?"

Mrs. Jones points toward the kitchen door and says, "In the garden. If picking corn out of the garden is going make you dream and sleep better, I will put your bed right in the middle of it and all your army buddies can join you. Um. I might just get me a pair of those army fatigues and join you."

Jacob gives out a hearty laugh and pauses for a moment and says, "Don't forget to get a pair for Melissa."

"Were you awake earlier? I thought I heard some popping sounds."

"Oh, that was just me messing around for a while before going back to sleep. Everything's okay."

"Good. I mess around some mornings myself. Not nearly as much as I used to.

Chapter 11

As the other members of the group start the next dream composition, Marcus sits with his head bowed and his hands wrapped around his mouth as tears gather in his eyes. He tries to fully absorb what has happened. Did he really make a dream composition for his brother that could possibly end the nights of torment? He looks at the solemn face of the Dream Master.

"Do you think that was enough to make a difference?" asks Marcus.

"We can only have a little faith."

"Yeah—that faith stuff."

The Dream Master touches Marcus on the shoulder and says, "That's all we have when we do our best to help and have no control over the outcome. That is the essence of you the dream maker."

Marcus opens his mouth to speak but only stares. He then rubs both eyes with his hands. He shakes his head and blinks his eyes rapidly as though he is having trouble seeing.

As he stares again at the Dream Master, he remembers the Dream Master's words.

"I'm so sleepy—no fooling. Is there something you need to tell me now that you wouldn't tell me earlier when I asked about sleep?"

The Dream Master only stares at him for a moment with a smile. "Yes. It's time for you to move on. I didn't tell you earlier, because I didn't know how long you would be with me."

"So, this is it?"

"I think so, Mr. Jones. I must help you to the tunnel right away. You don't want to miss your ride, do you?"

"Do you need any help?" asks Miguel.

"No. Thanks."

The Dream Master leads Marcus out of the theater to the tunnel. Marcus is so sleepy that he can barely stand without assistance. When they arrive at the tunnel, Marcus steps in and falls to his knees with his arms folded on top of his head.

"This is it?" says Marcus.

"Yes. Just turn and face the other way."

Marcus slowly turns on his knees. The tunnel activates, and he raises his hands above his head. This time Marcus sees no sparkling lights but only walls of crystal blue and the bright light at the end. He feels himself moving and spreads his arms further upward as he lifts his head high with a smile. The Dream Master stands outside the tunnel with his hands clasped at his chest. Marcus's group rush into the foyer and see the Dream Master standing alone and Marcus inside the activated tunnel. The Dream Master nods to them with a smile as Marcus fades into the light and shouts, "Lord, I'm here!"

And back at 4202 Castle Drive, Jacob Jones appears to be engaged once again in a vivid demonstration of whistle-snoring. Mrs. Jones approaches the doorway of his bedroom and listens for a while. She knocks and receives no answer. She enters and looks around the room and sees that everything is still in place. She very quietly approaches Jacob and sits on the edge of the bed.

"Boo!" he says as he snaps around to look at her. "I am a trained soldier, you know."

"You sure caught me. I wanted to remind you of your evaluation at the VA today."

"Thanks. I didn't set the clock, because I didn't think I would sleep all night. I thought the other restful night was just luck."

"Well, you slept well and loudly. My Jacob is back."

"I had a pleasant dream again, even though it was still a little about war. You always said that you just have to wait for the change to come."

"Change takes time. You have to expect it, recognize it, and be prepared for it."

"I wish Marcus was here so he could also get a good night of sleep."

"He's resting now."

They hear a knock at the front door. Mrs. Jones leaves to answer, and Jacob rises to shower and dress. She greets Melissa, who enters with a fast-food tray with coffee and biscuits, which she takes to the kitchen table.

"I'm early, but you don't have to fix breakfast. I brought something for us to eat before I leave with Jacob. Is he getting ready?"

"Yes, and he should be well rested for the doctor after a night of snoring. His PTSD is now post-traumatic snoring disorder."

"He can make some noise."

"Yeah, but it sounded good to me. I can live with it. I might have snored a little myself now that I can truly get some rest. But he made another sound. It was a popping sound. It was like poppity pop, pop, poppity pop, poppity pop. It was a repetition. I couldn't figure out what it was. He said he was just messing around."

"Maybe he was practicing a secret code or something. You know, like Morse code. It has dot dot dashes. Maybe he was beating on the desk. Does he rap?"

"Jacob? No. Maybe it was that Morse-code thing. I didn't want to be too nosy now that he is doing much better."

They hear Jacob emerge from the bedroom. He is dressed in pressed army khaki pants and an army khaki shirt with an open collar. He is wearing a white T-shirt under the khaki shirt, and a few links of the chain of his identification tag are protruding from under the T-shirt. The pressed pants and shirt are complimented by the glossy black army dress shoes from the closet. Mrs. Jones and Melissa are surprised that he has replaced the combat boots and camouflage fatigues with the semiformal outfit. It is not the desired dress for his new civilian life, but it is a start. Mrs. Jones walks to him with a smile and tucks the exposed chain under the T-shirt and then gently presses down the ends of his collar with her hands. After she finishes, Jacob stands erect as though he is being inspected by a commanding officer. Mrs. Jones also stands erect in front of him and looks him straight in the eyes. Then she looks down at his shoes.

"I've never seen shoes shine like that before."

"Oh, that was the noise you might have heard at night."

"Oh, your rag shining your shoes?"

"Yes, ma'am. The rag makes the popping sound, and the sound makes the shine."

"What?"

"If you can't make the pop, you can't make the shine."

"Oh, I see. It's just like your mouth makes the snores, and the snores put a shine on my face."

"Ha! I guess something like that."

"Well, guess what, Mr. Army man. This evening the three of us are going to the movies, and you will have to stay awake."

He looks at Melissa and states, "Oh, one of those kinds of movies—no car chases, no violence, and no alien attacks. It will be like seeing the shrink."

"Don't call your psychiatrist a shrink after all he has tried to do for you. Look at you now—all cheery and stepping more like a soldier."

"Maybe he helped a little. But I believe it's more you and that faith stuff."

"Faith!" exclaims Mrs. Jones.

"That's what I said—that faith stuff."

"Don't worry, Jacob," says Melissa. "If you need some action at the movies, there will be plenty of popcorn."

"Popcorn?" he asks.

Afterword

The Veterans Administration (http/tsd.va.gov/public/problems/nightmares.asp) states,

> Nightmares are one of the symptoms of PTSD. For example, a study comparing Vietnam Veterans to civilians showed that 52% of combat Veterans with PTSD had nightmares fairly often. Only 3% of the civilians in the study reported that same level of nightmares. Other research has found even higher rates of nightmares.

Jacob Jones represents a multitude of war veterans who suffer with post-traumatic stress disorder. Fortunately his condition could be manipulated by fictitious events. The difficulty in treating combat PTSD is the need for managing the flow of thoughts and emotions from combat trauma that is in some cases constantly fed by the flow of thoughts and emotions from negative situations in civilian life. That is why treatment for PTSD requires all the elements portrayed in this story—the undying support of family and friends, quality professional care, patience, and faith.

ABOUT THE AUTHOR

Elmer Haygood is a graduate of Hardin-Simmons University in Abilene, Texas, and a retired Human Services Supervisor for the Family and Aging Services of Hillsborough County, Florida, that includes Veteran Affairs. He is the author of The Cross Trap and They Came to Heal Us and lives in Tampa, Florida.

Printed in the United States
By Bookmasters